# TRANSMORPHOSIS

*&*

## Other
## Short
## Story

Boris Belony

Boris Belony

Stitchy Press First Edition 2009

For more information please contact
www.StitchyPressHQ.com

Printed on recycled paper
Printed in Wales by Cambrian Printers
Body Copy set in 10 on 13pt Sabon
Headlines set in 22pt Amarillo USAF
(with a whopper outline)

Illustration by Mike Ahern
*www.TeamDaddy.com*
Design by Karl Toomey
*www.KarlToomey.com*

ISBN 978-0-9561317-0-6
This is Stitchy Press SP006

Stitchy
press

# ACKNOWLEDGEMENTS

I'd like to acknowledge the following people for their contribution: Natalia, Willie, Mike, Karl, Julia, Cian, Ailbhe, Claire, Paddy, Eoin, James, Noreen, Ronan, Ed, Kim, Naomi, Turlough, Hazel, Isabel, de folks. I'd also like to thank God for creating everything; like language, computers, humour, creativity, cognition, matter and existence. Without it, none of this would even be possible.

# CONTENTS

# SNIFFING WATER

I ran over to the football and stabbed it deep in its heart with my fork.[1] It bled a stream of air and fell from my grasp. Stupid football won't land in my garden again, I thought and threw the corpse over the wall to the children playing next door.

I walked back into my house and put some cigarettes in the toaster. The smell of fag–smoke was always a sure way to calm me down. I opened a press to look for some food. It was three in the afternoon and I hadn't eaten for at least two days. A couple of tins of Canelli beans and a tub of ketchup were all that met my eyes. I went out to the freezer. It was empty apart from an exploded can of Fosters and some bag-less peas spread around in the ice. I took a knife out of the drawer and scraped them out into my hand. I put the ketchup, beans and peas into a pan and started to fry them up. As the ingredients cooked, I heard my immersion calling to me.[2] I ran up the stairs and breathlessly opened the hot press door.

'You ok?' I asked the insulated container.

'No, I'm hungry,' it replied.

'Well I'm just in a process of making some lunch, I'll be up with it soon'.

'Ha, ha' it said. 'You know I can only eat watts.'

---

1. This is the first line of my book.
2. Internal broiling/heating system in a house. Some call it 'the focus of the home.'

I looked at it glumly.

'Yes I know, I'm sorry – I'll go and try get some electricity now.'

I went down, turned off the pan and brought it out into the back garden, flinging the sizzling food over the wall at the children playing ball. That'll serve them right, I chuckled and left my house in search of some watts. I stood in my estate, looking around for somewhere or somehow I could get some electricity.

'Where are you oh sauce of modern life?' I enquired, hoping an enchanted cat or rabbit might aid me in my quest. But no such beast was to appear to me today. I walked over to a small green box sitting outside a neighbour's house. 'Danger: Keep Away' it said under a yellow triangle which contained a black symbol of electricity. I was sure that this contained some volts. I kicked at it, but it was sturdier than it looked. I walked into the neighbour's garden and picked up a rock from a flower bed in front of their sitting room window. I smashed it down onto the box with all my might, creating a decent crack to appear. Just then the neighbour appeared from their house.

'What the fuck do you think you're doing?' he cried.

'It's none of your business Oisin!' I yelled back.

He came right up to me and started gesticulating wildly.

'Have you gone completely mad?! I'm calling the guards! I've had it up to here with your wild behaviour! You're out of control and a danger to decent people living near you!'

Anger detonated within me.

'You don't fucking know three things about madness!!

You don't know forty things about madness!! What you think is mad another thinks logical, what I think is mad another thinks natural!!! Sanity is perception my friend. And it looks like you're having some sort of perception drought!!! If I told you that this green box was red there's no way in Santry you could prove it to me. Ha ha, so you see, through the powers of human reasoning I have reduced your argument to a sneering dribble![3] I need the juice from this lecky box and there's nothing you can do about it!'

'You're a fucking maniac, I'm calling the guards!' he shouted and stormed off.

I picked up the rock and threw it at him, catching him on the back of his neck. There was a deep 'thuck' sound and he fell to the ground. I got back to my work with even more gusto, kicking the box frantically.

Finally, the plastic covering gave way and I got a glimpse of the works inside. I dug my hands into the wires and started tugging. Oisin was hobbling into his house now, holding onto the back of his neck and some more neighbours were watching from their doors. As I pulled, I felt a sudden jolt and flash of pain and then confusion. A second later, I was lying on the grass beside the box, breathless. A few wires were sparking and spitting. I must be full of electricity now, I thought and picked myself up and stumbled back to my house.

I ran in the front door and up to my immersion. The sight which greeted me was horrendous. The tank had been chopped in with an axe or something and the insulation lagging was scattered all over the place.

'Are you still alive??!' I yelled, but there was no

---

3. Clever philosophical tactic which opens up so many existentialist questions. There's no way you can prove to someone that you both see the same colour. Their red could be your blue. If there's no way of proving what colour you're seeing then how can you prove rice exists?! Or lipstick, or frost, or anything for that matter?!! I always pull this card out when faced with a sticky argument.

answer. The immersion was dead. I began weeping uncontrollably. Outside, sirens were fading in to blare on the street. Who could have done such a thing to me?? Who could have smashed up my immersion??? I lay, face down onto the sodden carpet and started biting the strands in despair. Someone started knocking hard on the door.

'Gardai – open up!'

'No!' I replied into the carpet.

After another few moments and more banging, I lifted my head and urinated in shock at what I saw. Scrawled in fat on the landing wall was:

*this is wat u get for throwing a pan at us cunt–dik. hope yr sad.*

That I was. Oh that my friends, I was.

# THE DIET

A couple of weeks ago I got an horrendous shock when I discovered I was pathologically overweight. I stood on the scales in my bathroom completely shocked.

'Nine stone??!' I screamed into my toothbrushes and Lynx. 'That's disgusting!! I have to buy a pair of black drainpipes today!'

I leapt off the damning scales and walked around in a panicked sweat. Maybe it was just a dream, I thought and poured some Toilet Duck into my eyes to awaken myself. When I arrived back from hospital I decided I needed to go on a diet and fast – but which one? So many claim to have the answer – Atkins, Dr. Gillian, Special K, Weight Watchers, Anorexia, Slim–Fast, Slimming World, Ecstasy, Paisean Fasiean, Carol Vorderman, so goddamn many options!!!

To start off I decided to cut out food altogether and drink only salt. After another brief hospital visit and a pallet of anti–depressants I realised I needed something a little more wholesome. Maybe I could bleed some of the weight out! I took a knife from the kitchen, made two slits under my armpits and tried to soak out some unwanted weight with Bounty kitchen paper. After a period of fairly sustained agony I ran upstairs excitedly to check the scales!

'What?!' I shouted. 'Twelve Stone??!!' Then I

suddenly realised I was standing on a clock!!! How could I have been so stupid??!! I had never been nine stone at all!!! I had been looking at nine – the time!!! I wept with relief, thanking God that awful nightmare was over. Later, as I picked at the scabs under my arms I thought of Dove Soap[4] and realised how lucky I was to be naturally beautiful again.

4. Dove soap.

# TRANSMORPHOSIS

Just like the main character in Kafka's allegorical murder/
mystery *Metamorphosis*, I didn't wake up quite like myself
one morning! I opened my eyes on the morning in question
and was alarmed to discover I had transformed into a giant
Silverfish overnight.

I looked down at my disgusting silver body
and tried to figure out what had happened to me!
Everything had been normal the night before,
I had brushed my tooth, watched some UFC on
Bravo and then fell quickly to sleep. I only woke
up once during the night, to get a drink of strange
purple liquid I found in an old phial in my attic.
But somehow I was now lying on my bed as a
silverfish, about the size of a sleeping bag filled
with leaves.

I scuttled off my bed and headed for the door but
realised I was far too short to reach the handle. Cursing
loudly in a strange inhuman voice, I knocked a glass statue
to the ground to get the attention of my family downstairs.
It smashed loudly and almost immediately I heard footsteps
running up the stairs. The noise of the moving feet had a
queer effect on me and I felt an overwhelming urge to hide
that instant! I looked around, panicking, my wiry feelers
desperately trying to seek out a nook to squeeze into. The
gap under my bed seemed like the only likely place. This is

madness I thought, I need to talk to them to explain what has happened to me! But logic was taking a back seat and my gut feeling to hide was in control. I slid under the bed, my feelers burning in terror. I could hear the footsteps reaching the door and then my mother's voice.

'Is everything OK in there? We heard a crash, oh I hope you are OK and are not in trouble!' I wanted to answer, but was still painfully afraid to come out from under the bed or even make a sound.

'Oh he's not answering!' She cried. 'Oh but why won't you answer, you must answer!' she continued.

Then I heard my father speak. 'Son, what has happened? Why don't you answer to your mother?! Is it necessary to enter by force to assess your safety?!'

'Oh please open the door Douglas and see if he's alright!' begged my mother.

'He may be masturbating with headphones on!' replied my father sternly. 'I don't want to cause a monsoon of embarrassment!' Just then the door opened and my panic went into overdrive. I started trying to eat down into the carpet to get away. My jaws were far more powerful than I expected and the carpet tasted delicious. My parents quietly called my name.

'Are you in bed, I see your statue is apiece, what has happened? Why don't you reply?!' asked my father.

'What is that ghastly noise?' enquired my mother with fear. 'It seems to be coming from beneath the bed!'

Oh cunt! I thought and started eating even faster, biting through the boards now.

'Fetch my rifle,' ordered my father and my mother promptly ran from the room. My eyes were bulging in terror and my head turned rapidly from side to side in desperate agitation. The hole in the floor was too small, it was only about seven inches across – I'd never escape through it! The door! It's the only escape! In a flash, I raced out from under the bed and scurried out the door as quick as I could.

My vision was too poor to make anything out, but my feelers did my work for me. I could hear my father shrieking in the bedroom behind me. As I hurried down the stairs I could hear my mother screaming now.[5]

'Shoot the thing!' yelled my father. But my mother was too busy howling. I ran towards the front door in wild panic and smashed into it headlong. I screamed in a loud horrifying wail, making my parents even more manic. My mind was barely functioning for fear. I dashed back down the hall, into the kitchen and towards the back door. Now I could hear my little sister joining in the excitement.

'Get him with the tea!' shouted my mother. 'Get him with that scalding tea you're making!' My sister could do nothing but scream. Luck ejaculated all over me as I found the back door wide open. I scampered out and into the sunlight which felt utterly painful and uncomfortable. I made my way quickly to the side of the house and paused to gather my bearings.

I became aware of a large shape looming in front of me. I could hear it emitting a deep, angry growl. It was Fungus, the family dog! Christ!! Luck had just set me up for a double cross! I had always had a good relationship with Fungus and hoped to fuck she could smell some sort of remnant of me. I tried to call her name, but the noise came out more like a terrifying saxophone blast. Fungus

---

5. My mother had a wail like a speared maggot!*

*Speared on a needle I suppose.

reacted immediately and jumped at me snarling, her jaws snapping and biting at me. I screamed and tried to escape but she was holding me with her claws. Pain erupted as she savaged through one of my feelers and then a leg. The attack was relentless.

'Fungus, no!' I screamed, but again, it sounded nothing like words. My only chance was to desperately try to fight back. I positioned my jaws and gave it a shot. In an instant, my powerful teeth had sliced her head clean off. Fungus slumped to the ground, her head rolling across the patio and coming to a stop at a wheelbarrow. I could hear my parents coming out the door, so I dashed off again to avoid having to hear any more of their distress.

I bolted out to the front driveway and across the road. I narrowly escaped a collision with a car and frantically raced into the cover of a nearby field, not stopping until I had reached the relative safety of a thick hedge. I stayed there a long time, nursing my wounds and trying to get to grips with what exactly I had become.

In the months that followed, that hedge was to become my home, a base from which I went out foraging for food, eating mice, shrews, cats and the odd child. My emotions and thoughts soon adapted to life as a Silverfish, but I could never fully succeed in battling the crushing loneliness that accompanied such a solitary existence. Once I thought I had come across another like me, but it just turned out to be a bag of cement half hidden in the grass. I get through my days hoping to find an antidote to my condition, or at least an answer. But I know I may never find it. If I don't try however, I may as well toss myself off a cliff and sail into the crashing surf below.

# REJECTION

I was cleaning up tables in a restaurant one day when the owner told me to get out.

'Who the fuck are you anyway??!' he screamed as he threw my Domestos out after me. Grumpily I put my stuff back into a plastic bag and walked off down the street. Where will I go now? I pondered and after a few moments of polite consideration I decided upon Tower Records. No one gives a shit how long you hang around in there, I thought and walked in that direction.[6] Upon arrival I was denied entry at the door by a plain clothed security creep.

'What's a big idea?!' I cried, trying desperately to compose myself and look real.

'You're not coming in here,' said the vile savage. 'You were kicked out of here last week for masturbating behind a jazz rack.' Appalled at this outrageous accusation I reproached him for his erroneous remark.

'You're wrong,' I informed him, 'I'm from Thailand and have never even been in this shop!'

'Bullshit,' replied the ape. 'You're name's Larry Longway and I'm your brother. I threw you out of this place by the dick myself last Wednesday!' I stood there disgusted at the way this brute was treating me.

'Well then, I'm off to get a guard, you'd

---

6. This shop seems to be fitted out specifically to deal with the lost soul. At the rear end of the shop it has bean bags and couches intended for the weary hole. If you can manage to scare off the rabble of wretched teens that might be hanging around them, you can be guaranteed a fairly pleasant day.

better get some proof!' With that I marched off, but as soon as I turned the corner I slumped down defeated. Why did that prick have to be working today? I thought in silence and made my way up to HMV. They had no secluded jazz racks but at least the staff were too afraid to stop me caressing my twig openly in the classical section.

# CONSIDERATION OF A HOUND

I walked home from yoga the other day to see all my friends arsing around in my front garden on stilts![7] The ignorant fucks! Big holes all over the garden and neighbour's phoning pigs left, right and centre! How would they like it if I strode around to their gaff and rolled around in their flower beds?

---

7. Something tells me this isn't the last I've heard of these guys!

# AH BUCK

I threw the rubber johnny on the ground in frustration, it just wouldn't obey.[8] I was angry. Angry at my mum, angry at meat eaters and angry at the johnny. Why couldn't it just focking open? It's not like I was a snivelling little runt begging it to open politely and lacking totally in confidence!! I had commanded! Commanded the prick to open, but it was as stubborn as a lake. I had even considered magic but I knew that wouldn't get me to anywhere.

---

8. There's nothing worse than the smell of johnny-smoke.

# RABIES

The rabies had me good. Very good. I tried to think, but all that came to my head was a sketch of dinosaurs. It was an extremely hot thought and bent away into a terrifying concept I can't describe because I know you won't understand it. I needed help and kept trying to clear my head, but it was no use – this deliriously ill man with gnashing jaws was on a road to *PomPAI(N)!*

It had all started three weeks earlier when I had been caving in a Dart tunnel and had eaten some jam I found discarded by the track. It must have contained the rabies virus because two weeks later I was attacking my friends with swords made from my arms and trying to eat anything that looked like an 's'. Even my own dog was afraid of me and was pissed off when I tried to eat its tail.

My life was deteriorating as rapidly as my control over my central nervous system. Nothing was the same as before. When I left my house the birds insulted me with scandalous language, houses looked like fax machines and the cars like brooches. My mind was flapping in the wind like a brick wall. I needed help, and not slowly.

I somehow managed to make it into my doctor one evening and begged the receptionist for help. Foam sprayed out of my mouth as I tried to explain I was unwell. I even swallowed my phone to convince them.

Within hours I was rushed into a doctor's room and examined.

'You either have rabies or *Voliosis*!' she told me.[9] 'Go to a hospital and see.'

They called a medical taxi for me and I was sped to the local hospital and seen immediately, relatively. Blood, urine, statements and saliva were all taken. I can't really remember too much of it now, but I do remember attacking the vending machine in the waiting room and biting out a young girl's throat. For some reason the blood excited me, but I could only bring myself to drink a few centilitres. I was treated slightly differently after that, first sedated with some fists and then invited into a coma with a fire extinguisher.

After a long and rather uneventful coma I finally awoke to the frankly depressing revelation that the girl was quite dead and I was to be charged with manslaughter. The bright side however was that the coma had caused my brain to partially shut down, protecting it from the virus while my body built up an immunity. I had survived the rabies!

I tried pointing this out to the parents of the girl but they were unimpressed and the judge sentenced me to pay them a large sum of money for their distress. I managed to escape jail because I had not been in full control of my faculties at the time of the incident, but it was a close call.[10] Of course, what I

---

9. I can't be quite sure whether she said this or not. I've searched the internet since and rung nearly every doctor in the 01 phone book looking for information on *Voliosis*, but I've come up with nothing. Was I hallucinating? The doctor also said "stop urinating in my face" and I definitely did urinate, towards her face anyway.

10. My first lawyer was a man called Michael Strand. He was useless. He tried getting me off by saying I wasn't even at the scene at the time of the incident,

that I had been mending his chimney. All the evidence stood against this claim however; CCTV footage, mobile phone video recordings and sworn statements by everyone involved (including me). It was even captured with crystal clarity on 35 mm film by a film crew who happened to be shooting a documentary at the scene. The judge had the lawyer arrested for perjury and I was given another legal aid, Greta Goblin. She was much better and instead explained that I had been in the throws of a brain melting illness.

didn't tell them was that, just like the jam by the railway, a little part of me had enjoyed it.

# STRAW

The thought occurred to me the other night that if we were all made of straw so many more people would die of fire. I put down the needle and tourniquet and lay back on my mattress to ponder this thought and ruminated on it for a good day or so. I concluded that humans couldn't ever be made out of straw, even if there was no such thing as fire. For instance, straw wouldn't be able to form complex working structures like a brain or the organs necessary to run one. Straw could never evolve into a moving, thinking being which could build houses, hunt animals or even communicate. Even if there were prehistoric humans made of straw they would soon become an evolutionary dead end. Ask any anthropologist worth his/her... straw (!!) if they would out-evolve flesh 'n' blood humans. All an ancient caveman would have to do is douse the cunt in flames or flatten him with a rock/ branch etc. Interesting theory, but I won't be submitting it to Nature journal just yet!

# GLASS WAR

I was once made of glass and it was NO PICNIC. It all started at the smelting works. My master was a lowly smeltsman named Gilly and one day when he was in the pub, a mysterious man offered to sell him an old antique grandfather clock. Always on the sniff for a good deal, Gilly accepted and paid the man forty pounds for the thing. He brought it back home on a sack–truck and put it in his bathroom, beside the toilet. He sat down to take a shit when the clock began to chime. He looked up with a start to see it was twelve. Midnight. Suddenly the clock began to speak.

'Reach inside my works or I'll reduce you to ash you smelting cunt!' It boomed.

'Oh lord – please deliver me from this satanic clock!' wailed Gilly, afraid out of his brain.

'Stop that snivelling you wretch!' shouted the clock. 'There is no God – only spooks, spirits and other entities you can't comprehend! Now reach into my works you fillet of filth!'

Terrified, Gilly stood up, his penis dangling modestly like a boiled pasta tube. He walked over and opened the clocks chest, revealing loads of cogs and wheels, all whirring and ticking rhythmically.

'What can I do sire?' asked Gilly with a trembling voice.

'Turn the Sonnet Cog and then wind my Havana

Bolt', replied the clock. Too scared to ask what they were, Gilly began to turn loads of different wheels and shit. There was a loud crunching sound and the clock began to scream.

'Nooooooooooo!!!!!' it yelled. 'What have you done??!!'

There was a huge bang, like forty black cats going off at once, and then a bright flash of light. The toilet was full of smoke and Gilly had to open the door to see anything. The clock was gone and in its place sat a little pile of ashes.

'I must get rid of these enchanted ashes!' said Gilly and swept them into an envelope.

The next day in work at the Smelting Works he sprinkled the ash into the molten glass, hoping it would break the spell. But as Newton said in *Principia*[11]; "something that is created can never be destroyed," and I was born – a fully glass human. A week later I turned normal.

---

11. Have never read the cunt. Never will either.

# ETHEREAL AND
# PISSED OFF

Nobody knows how shit it is to be a ghost. I'm transparent, misunderstood, strange, frightening, old, bored, useless, starved of attention, intangible, supernatural and sad. All I get to do all day is float around the place looking at newspaper headlines and going into people's homes imagining being normal again like them. I had a life once, but I was killed by my wife for not cleaning the shed. The bitch cut my head off with an axe and hid it behind some boxes of cereal in Tesco. The police eventually captured her after they were called when she tried to put one of my legs in a freezer in a small Asian supermarket. I like to go and blow on her face in prison - it drives her crazy! Oh well, ain't (no) life a spook?

# HOLDING OUT
# FOR A HERO

Graham Spar was as excited as a bitch in heat. It was Christmas Eve and he was standing in his Christmas tree waiting nervously for Santa to arrive with festive pressies. As he stood in amongst the branches, he breathed in deeply through his nose, the smell of pine needles reminding him strongly of Christmas. It was just after midnight and he was sure Santa would arrive soon. He looked at the time on his laptop in the corner of the room and waited.

He had tried the experiment a few times in his youth but had never succeeded in encountering the elusive gift giver. It didn't help that his parents had both been alcoholics who delighted in teasing him about his love for Santa, calling him a faggot day and night for most of the advent period.

'Hoping Santa will drop by with a few gifts do you?' his Father would ask in a wretched teasing voice. 'Well he won't, your boyfriend doesn't exist, so stop being so faggy and give up thinking about him!'

His mother was no better, calling Santa a paedophile in "sad, red clothes." She suffered from several mental disorders, all voluntary, and regularly walked around the house on Christmas day wearing nothing but a few watches. Despite his parent's hostility towards Santa, Graham still had reason to believe in him. Every Christmas morning, he would find a sock hanging from the ceiling in his sitting room with gifts in it for him. Sometimes they were shit ones like walnuts or wooden toy soldiers, but he loved them all nonetheless.[12] Knowing that his parents would never give him such things confirmed his belief in the mythical Christmas man and every passing year made him want to meet him even more. All his previous attempts had failed in one way or another. Either he had waited in the wrong house, ended up being hospitalised with anxiety, or even once, had fallen asleep! He could feel it in his bones that this time was going to be different and that he would meet with his hero soon.

Another twenty minutes passed and Graham began to get peckish. Some foil wrapped chocolates hung tantalisingly from the branches which he desperately wanted to devour, but he didn't move for fear of making himself more visible. The room sat quiet and dark, the fairy lights from the tree sprinkling colour across the walls.

A green light hung irritatingly close to his eye.

A *Tesco Value Mince Pie* and glass of *Super Milk* sat expectantly on a little table, awaiting Father Christmas's lips.

Dust sat behind the TV, profoundly unaware of anything, even Christmas.

Graham stood and tried to push the excitement in his chest away. Butterflies was too mild a word, he thought, more like dragons! Or Rocs! Every second seemed to stretch into one and a half seconds! He tried not to think of his possible imminent encounter, but images of him and Santa laughing and shaking hands made him need to poo with anticipation.

---

12. Á la *Mr. Kipling* ads or very old cartoons.

Suddenly he heard a noise from the chimney. A sort of scraping, scratching sound. He glanced over at the laptop. It was 12:35. His heart started thumping. His eyes stared at the fireplace, watching for any sign of movement. The scratching got louder. Graham wanted to scream, but held his voice in. Then he noticed a movement in the fireplace, something was coming down from the chimney! He watched as a shape fell into the grate and then pulled itself into the room. This is it, he thought, this is the moment!! In an instant he ran to the light switch and filled the room with light. Then Graham screamed in horror.

Standing before him was a small goblin–like creature about 3 feet in height. It wore dirty brown robes and had long, wiry white hairs sprouting from around its mouth like whiskers. It's yellow and red eyes were wide with fright and it made a terrible gurgling sound from its throat.

'Begone vile fiend!' yelled Graham and picked up a short sword from the sofa.

'Wait!' warbled the disgusting creature, its sneering lips revealing a rotting mouth with black teeth. 'Do not slay me, for I am Santa Claus!'

'No!' screamed Graham. 'Don't lie to me! Santa is a jolly cunt with a big white beard and red clothes!! You are but a ghoul!'

'Hence why I refuse to be seen by little childers, case I scare their poor souls! I may look like a demon but I have a heart of gold! Appearances deceive the mind, I am full of benevolence and –'

The creature could say no more for Graham had stuck

the short sword deep into its face. Thick, black blood oozed out from around the protruding blade. Graham pulled the sword out and kicked the body into the tree in horror. It was dead.

After taking a few seconds to recover, Graham turned off the light and shakily climbed back into his hiding place. He looked down at the foul body and something caught his eye. A piece of material sticking out of what looked like a pocket. He bent down to investigate further. It looked familiar. He pulled it out of the pocket and his heart stopped. His stocking. His Christmas sock that appeared on the ceiling every year. Complete with a small gift of some marbles. 'Oh my Christ,' whispered Graham. 'I just killed Sir Claus.'

He began to sob and hugged the little body. How could he have done it? How could he have committed this unimaginable act? Tears streamed down his face as he held Santa in his arms. What of all the people who will no longer receive the gift of Santa?! All the people who bravely held onto their beliefs about this most magnanimous and generous of beings! What of the very spirit of Christmas?!

As Graham grappled with these questions it slowly dawned on him what he had to do. In a moment of divine epiphany he embraced his destiny.

'I am Santa,' he whispered. 'I am Santa.'

Moments later he was putting on the grimy brown robes and thinking about the task ahead of him. 'I have a lot of work to do!' he laughed and walked to the front door. He took one more look behind him at his fallen hero and left the house to deliver presents to everyone. But he only made it a kilometre or so before collapsing and dying with nervous exhaustion.

# THE BIG BANG

I bit into the balloon and it burst.

'What in God's name was that snap?!' screamed my grandmother from the other room.

'It wasn't a snap grandmother!' I replied curtly. 'It was a bang.'

'Well it sounded like a snap to me!' she screamed in return.

'Well I'll bet you a hundred euro it wasn't!' I shouted.

'Are you sure? I thought I heard a loud snap!'

'Granny - It wasn't a snap, get over it. I bit a balloon and it burst. That's all. A snap doesn't describe that sound well at all!! Think of a balloon bursting and then think of bending a red Coca Cola ruler till it breaks. Two very different sounds as your memory will tell you.'

There was silence for a moment.

'I think it was a snap!'

'A thousand trumpets Gran!! Eat some more Omega-3 fatty acids you mad bitch, you're deficient in so many ways!!!

Suddenly a horrible thought exploded in the outer reaches of my brain. Now that I think of it, it did sound more like a snap!! Oh my god!! I was utterly wrong. I wheeled my wheelchair as fast as I could down to the newsagents and bought a box of Quality Street with undisguised panic. I wheeled back home ar nós na gaoithe and showered my Gran with the sweets and apologies.

# THE SWIMMING POOL

Word was spreading that a giant had been seen walking around a nearby town called Pore. People were excited, but also scared. What if the great thing came stumbling into our neck of the woods? What if it was walking around our village? The thought of being safe and cosy in your house while the lumbering hulk trudged around Pore was actually quite comforting. You'd lie there under your patchwork quilt and imagine watching the fascinating beast walking around, as tall as a house! Sometimes you'd imagine him looking at you! People only ever did that while safe and warm in bed.

Imagining the giant looking at you was the scariest thing! Imagine! If I had been out cutting wood and looked up only to see a giant looking at me, I'd have surely dropped like a sack of grain with the fright. But the giant was in Pore, or so people said. I was out drinking from the village well when my friend Klit walked over. I could sense him brimming with a very real excitement.

'Hiya!' he said brightly. 'Hear the news 'bout giant in Pore?'[13]

'Surely did, 'twas in every mouth down tavern till dusk!' I replied.

Klit clasped his hands together and rubbed them, watching me as I drank. Then he blurted it right out. 'Y'see, me an' the boys got thinkin'. What if we go Pore

---

13. Ah, Pore!

and see giant for ourself! It'd be fun as an ox to see giant in Pore!'

'An' mighty dangerous!' I replied swiftly. 'You don't want go 'round messin' with giant. Specially not some giant in Pore! Who know what giant do? Could eat your head off and use your arms as paddles for some boat!' Klit looked down disappointedly. To tell the truth, I wanted nothing more than to go to have a sneaky look at this giant, but I'm one of those people who constantly points out the negative aspects of any idea and suggest it doesn't go ahead even though I want to do it as much as anyone. Luckily this time Klit was determined enough to push me.

'Fuck 't!' he said. 'If you don't go, I'll kill that young un!' He pointed at a dead child on the path.

'That un's 'ready dead Klit you dot–brain! But ok I'll come along – just so's you not going do somethin' stupid!'

Klit jumped in the air and spun around in glee. 'We goin' to a giant!'

An hour later myself and two friends Silk and Silc were on our way to Pore. Klit couldn't make it as he had fallen into a fever and died, but we took one of his hairs along as a reminder of him. It didn't take long to reach the first buildings of Pore. It was an uneventful journey, but we had kept a keen eye a watch all around us, in case the giant had migrated towards our village. The streets were empty and an eerie silence hung over the usually-quiet-enough-anyway town. I threw a stone into a shop and Silc looked for some beer. Then a moment later I heard a loud shuffling sound from a street nearby.

'Silk!' I hissed. ''Tis most likely giant!' We jumped into an empty swimming pool and watched with our eyes peeking slightly over the edge. Then we saw him. A giant, as tall as the house! He walked slowly and with quite some effort. Silk dived down into the pool out of sight, but my curiosity glued me to him. I watched as he moved, his arms swinging slowly by his side. After a moment he was gone, walking off somewhere else. In my whole life, nothing has ever come close to that incredible experience.[14]

---

14. That may be a tiny bit of a fib right there. There was another incredible experience I had that could certainly come close to that one. It happened some time after this incident and involved another giant. I was sitting in my house composing a piece of music, plagiarisingly similar to Bach's Prelude No 2 in C minor, when the village idiot came running past my window screaming about a giant in the nearby town of Brahm. I ran outside quickly, almost colliding with a friend of mine named Cif. 'Didn' ya hear oh didn' ya hear?' he asked excitedly. 'There a giant over in Brahm. Big un too! Bout size of a hundred fists!' He was excited. Very so. 'I got to thinkin,' he said. 'Maybe we could take peek at it over in Brahm, only for a wasp's sneeze, and then run all way back home, run the whole way back!' I explained the danger of the situation to him but he was far too eager. Eventually I relented and we were soon off on our way to Brahm with two other friends; Jale and Fuck. Before we even got there Jale had been killed stone dead by Fuck.

They had been quarrelling over a piece of fish so Fuck just threw him over the side of a cliff! I scolded him some. 'Fuck!' I said. 'Can't just go around throwin' peoples off cliff! You keep doin' that you won't have any peoples left and you be sittin' on your own in tavern, or goin see giant on your own!' He apologised and we moved on. When we got to Brahm it already seemed deserted. We decided to have a quick look around. Within a few moments I thought I could hear heavy footfalls. I peeked around a corner, but it was only Fuck beating Cif with a piece of cement. 'Oh Fuck you tick-tock! Leave Cif alone and be watchful for giant!' Fuck threw down the cement and helped a bloodied Cif onto his feet. Just then I did hear a sound of heavy feet. 'Boys!' I cried. 'Giant!' We all jumped down into a well and I managed to take a peek over the top and see the majestic giant walk past, unaware of my gaze. In a moment he was gone and I was reminded heavily of my time in Pore.

# THE POWER OF NOW
# AND NOW AND
# NOW AND NOW...

It was bright anyway. I looked out a window and saw some clouds hanging in the sky. Beyond them was more sky and then past that, night and stars and shit. I had just finished reading a popular psychology self–help book all about living in the moment and appreciating 'now'.[15]

I sat on my quilt and looked slowly around my room. I thought back to the book and how it advised to simply let your senses take in information and to enjoy it. My eyes. I will start with my eyes.

I opened them wide and peered around my room with joy. Clothes strewn around the ground, a broken Playstation 2, remains of an Indian take away, and a photograph of my girlfriend who had been killed in a crash the day before. I began to tremble with excitement. It was really working! I could feel the euphoria entering my body, from just looking around the place.

I switched to my hands and rubbed them across the cool sheets. I savoured the smooth softness of the cotton, allowing the sensation to fill my body. I picked at the crusty remains of glorious masturbation seizures, it all felt so wonderful. I might have been sticking my finger in the eye of a blowtorch and I wouldn't have noticed!

I pricked up my ears and listened carefully for any sounds that happened to vibrate my hear drum. A crow shouting at someone outside, the slight straining of the

---

15. I love popular psychology books. My favourites would probably be *Ascending from Suicidal to Bridal* (Smud, 1978) and *Defeat the Orc Within* (Balzac, 1990)

springs in my bed, the swish of water running down the pipes and hitting the drain outside, my wardrobe, the ring of a fly sailing about my room. It sounded like the most incredible orchestra the world has ever known! I felt faint with the bliss that was surging through me.

I took a deep breath through my nose and could smell my carpet, the unwashed clothes in a pile and the stale smell of my dead girlfriend's perfume, still hanging in the air. The smells caused my head to reel and I fell back onto the bed; looking, listening, feeling and smelling. My body was one lump of sense and my brain was the lucky cunt devouring it all. I smiled as I relished the oneness of my senses, but then suddenly realised that I was still utterly devastated and in complete despair over the death of my darling Katie.

# BLAST OFF

Melly always wanted to go to space. Ever since he was young he wanted to simply jump off the path and soar into the sky and out through the atmosphere. He longed to float through space and visit all the planets in our solar system and then, the mysteries beyond.

'Oh Papa!' he'd say. 'I'd love to sail off into space and visit distant moons!'

'Well you can't,' his Papa would say. 'You'd starve, die, burn, burst and blow up!! You need to be an astronaut and you never will.' His father was a tough man. Full of anger and resentment, he treated Melly like a weed. If he wasn't telling him he had no central nervous system, he was calling him a weed. Melly's mother was long gone. The only time Melly had ever met her was when he was being born. She left the hospital that day and was never seen again by people who knew her. Whenever Melly would ask his Pa where his mother was he would say 'dunno, distant galaxies maybe? Hopefully strayed too close to a sun!' This was what sparked Melly's fascination with space.

At the age of fifteen, Melly told his dad that he was going out to wash the car and ran down the road to a bus stop. Once there he jumped on the first bus heading to a space station. He was going to get to space no matter what. As soon as he arrived at the space station he broke in and went in search of a shuttle. Within a short time he found one in a massive warehouse. He quickly climbed up into the exhaust chamber and curled up to go asleep. Tomorrow is going to be the best day of my life, he thought before drifting off into a deep, restful snooze.

He was awoken the next day by a jolt. The craft was being taken to launch! He scurried further along the huge chamber and hid in a crevice in the floor. Snug in this little hideaway he could manage to stay put when the shuttle was put into position. After what seemed like a week it was ready for launch. He crossed his fingers as he heard the count down over the loudspeaker.

*5*
*4*
*3*
*2*
*1*

Lift Off!! Melly was reduced to ash in an instant.

# THE MIDDLE

And so we find ourselves in the middle of the book! Not the metric middle now, but the point which is not beginning, nor end, nor near either; in fact it is wholly superior to the metric middle! This is my favourite part of the book; here is where it all matters. Here is where the soul of the book nests!

Look into the side of the page there.

◀━━━

Don't tell me you can't feel a great power emanating from it!!

If you connect I want to hear about your experience. Let me know:

borisbelony@gmail.com

*or*

Boris B'l'n'
Stitchy Press
Drumnadubber
Drumsna
Co Leitrim

# BIRDS

I'll tell you something about motherfucking birds. The fucks come into my room every evening at the same time and chew through everything! So the other day on my way to a magazine shop I see one perched on a hedge >LOOKING< at me. I throw a pound at him but the fucker catches it!!

Birds – You can't sue 'em!

47

# THAT METEOR SHOWER

What's wrong with people who work in phone shops?? I went into a Meteor shop the other day as the phone I'd recently bought was broken. It was quiet enough when I walked in so I was attended to without much wait. So far so good.

'Howya goin' boss?!' Came the smart greeting from a blonde, razor–haired worker behind a counter.

'I'm fine – look will you fix my phone, it doesn't work at all,' I said, already losing patience with this overbearing ghoul.

'Just flick it onto the counter there man and we'll see if we can't find your problems!'

I cursed him inside my head and placed the phone on the counter.

'Eh that's not a phone it's a severed penis!' he said with horror. I looked down at the bloody lump sitting on the counter and screamed.

'Where did that come from??!' I yelled, picking it up and throwing it out the door.

'You just took it out of your pocket you mad bastard!' shouted the hysterical salesman. Then it dawned on me – my best friend Bastille who studies medicine in college must have placed it there as a practical joke.[16] I was about to explain when an old lady interrupted.

'Who threw this morsel of revulsion at my

---

16. Bastille never actually made it to the end of medicine. Half way through his final year at the RCSI he saw the film Phantasm. For some unknown reason he subsequently became obsessed with the paranormal. He quit medicine about three weeks before his final exams and bought a little cottage in Connemara where he now spends his time listening carefully to the wind to try and catch ghosts speaking to each other.

granddaughter??!' she cried with a shrill beam of voice.

'That would be me!' I started, raising my finger. 'But it was a medical error!' The old woman turned on me with a grey look of murder in her eyes.

'Well your medical error landed in my granddaughter's buggy!' she screamed.

'Please, you must understand, both of you. My friend Bastille Woolham is a medical student and he's always putting balls and tits and stuff in my pockets – he thinks it's as funny as Strauss, I however do not!!! Please accept my apology and let me buy your granddaughter a Mars drink,' I said, handing her a two euro piece. Seemingly satisfied enough with this, she exited without a further beam of noise.

I turned to the distressed salesman. 'Apologies, now can we please fix my phone and I'll be out of here without any more hassle.'

He looked at me for a moment and then replied.

'Ok, as long as you get rid of that thing properly.' He pointed at the nub of flesh the old lady had returned to the counter.

'Not a problem!' I laughed, walking out of the shop and in plain sight of the salesman dropped the item on the ground and crushed it enthusiastically with my foot. 'There!' I announced. 'Destroyed!'

I walked back in and placed my real phone on the counter. The man still looked upset as he picked it up. 'So what's wrong with it?' he asked, his verve visibly diminished.

'Well I keep hearing people laughing every time I ring up the girls on *Bangbabes* on Sky Digital Adult and I think it may have crossed lines or something,' I said.

'Bang what??!' He asked.

'Bangbabes' I replied. 'A service where you ring topless girls on TV and they talk to you while looking sexy. It's quite erotic. But anyway, I keep hearing people laughing when I chat with the babes.'

The salesman put down the phone. 'Look are you just completely taking the piss?'

'No!' I answered defensively. 'I just want you to fix my phone and stop the crossing lines. Can you fix it or not?!'

He just looked at me silently with an expression of deep cynicism. I picked up the phone and waved it around in front of his face to emphasis my sincerity. After thirty seconds or so I slammed the phone onto the counter.

'Fucking!' I shouted in exasperation.

'Look I think you'd better leave,' he said.

'What?!' I asked in horror.

'You have to leave, get out.'

I started banging the phone off my head in frustration. 'I'm not leaving till you fix my phone!!' I yelled.

'Mick, call Danny from upstairs will you, this nutjob's causing hassle,' said the salesman off into a backroom. He turned back towards me and scowled.

'No I'm not!!' I screamed, 'I just want to talk to the girls in peace!! I just want to know who in fuck is laughing as I explain sex fantasies to them!! I just want to talk to a sexy girl via phone while peering at them on a screen!!!'

It was too late. A person I can only assume was Danny came marching down a stairs so I ran out before he could shoot me. As a last ditch effort of defiance, I scooped up the remaining meat from the path outside and threw it in the door before running two miles and hiding in a Dart station jacks.

# CLOSURE

'Throw us nine logs there Polo!'

'No way Gus, last time I did that you threw four back!'

'Not a chance! Not this time Polo! You see, I'm saving. Not about to fuck several logs back at you!'

'Well you're a regular panto aren't you?!'

'Only as good as they're comin, only as good as they're comin! Ha ha! Now giz those logs Polo man!'

'They're on their way Gus, they're on their way!'

# THE BBQ MADE OF PAIN

I was having a BBQ with some friends a few nights ago when I confessed to a girl how much I loved her.[18] She was sitting down biting a vein off a chicken drumstick when I approached her.

'Hey Caoimhe, how are you doing?' I asked with a dollop of matter–of–fact.

'What?' she asked, pulling a part of the vein from between her front teeth. She put the miniature piece of tube on a tissue and looked at me with her delicious eyes.

'No, I was just asking how you are!' I said jovially. I was determined to come across as relaxed and confident. Girls want to be protected, I told myself and pushed my pelvis a little closer to her.

'Oh I'm fine', she said absentmindedly.

'Cool... What do you think of the meat on the barby, not bad eh?' I asked, tossing an Airwave into my gob.

'The meat... Oh I suppose it's dreamy – in a nightmarish kind of way.' She looked to her side, watching as our friend Melly took a piss against the shed. Every word she spoke was magic, how did she manage to make things sound so cool?!

'Look at Melly!' I laughed, 'He's taking a slash!'

She smiled and looked away. I wasn't going to let this trout escape!

---

18. I've always found it extremely hard to talk to girls. When I do pluck up the courage I usually just try to be funny, but I get really paranoid. I can never tell whether they're hysterically laughing at the jokes or not even smiling at all!

'Christ, it's a mild evening – do you want to walk to the shops to get a bar or something?'[19] I asked, looking at her directly and grabbing her arm forcefully to gain control.

'Let go of me!' she shouted and pulled her arm back.

'No Caoimhe, I think you should come to the shop,' I said holding her tighter.

'You're hurting me! Melly – do something, he's going crazy!!' She shouted. How dare she! The bitch!

The rascal! I struck her hard across her forehead, damaging my knuckles. She let out a shriek and in an instant Melly threw me to the ground, punching me repeatedly in the face. I watched as beautiful Caoimhe jumped up and ran from the plastic table and chairs, crying. I soon lost consciousness and awoke on the path outside Melly's house. Feeling surprisingly peckish I walked up to the Chinese and mulled over the incident at home with a Prawn Szechwan.

---

19. Can't remember now whether it was a Mars or a Fudge!

# CLIFFED

I was standing above a village called Fuddish Tite, which was nestled half way up an absurdly high cliff face. It was a sheer drop of many centimetres to the village from where I stood, and it was so far away I could only barely make out the people moving about below. The only way in or out of this place was death, birth or jumping, but no one had ever tried that as it meant certain death/death/ profound paralisation/or death. Nobody knew who had founded the village, how they built it or what the people who lived there even looked like! Binoculars did not work up here and even people with fantastic eyesight could not make out much apart from the vague shape of the buildings and the fact that there were people moving around. Where I stood was known as 'Spitter's Drop' because people would literally stand there for days or even weeks, spitting down upon the hapless villagers. Cunts, I used to think. Why would you do that?

The place filled me with curiosity and I was dying to know what it looked like. Judging by the distance to the village, I guessed I would be falling for about half a minute. I had a backpack full of gifts for the people; jam, herbs, paracetamol, lighters – that sort of thing. I had written a note too, explaining that I was planning on jumping and asking for them to make space for me to land. I had spent nearly twenty thousand euro getting it translated into over forty languages as I was unsure what language they spoke. I threw the bound bundle of pages over the side of the cliff and watched with dismay as the wind blew it a good half a kilometre in the wrong direction.

I cursed and cut myself in the arm with my penknife as punishment for missing.

'Fucking lunatic!' I screamed out into the air, and waited a few moments to calm down. I took an A4 page out of my bag and scribbled a quick note in English and French:

> *Hi kingdom of Fuddish Tite! I hav decided 2 visit u frm r wrld. Im friendly & rekon well get on grand!! Im going to drop in frm what u think is heaven maybe, but its not its jst the world. i hav so many things to ask u! Do u like gold? Do u believe in ghosts? Wat will u think wen I show u my i-phone etc. I havnt much space to write so expect me in about a min.'*

I made a little paper airplane out of the page and flung it with all my might at the village. Luck saluted me as the note sailed towards its destination and then gave me the finger as the airplane hit the cliff and burst into flames. I spat onto the ground about twenty times in anger, being careful not to send any over the edge. I tried sending the note another few times, once even writing less words to see if that would help, but every time it failed. Reluctantly, I got ready to jump without having sent the warning note. I walked up to the edge and peered over. It sure was some drop! I made sure my bag was tightly fitted to my back and walked off.

The first thing to go against plan was that I was falling head first instead of feet first. I tried to turn myself but was unsuccessful. As I fell closer, I suddenly realised that the village was actually just a gorse bush clinging to a rock shelf! I couldn't believe it! I looked again and realised I had just had my eyes closed and that the gorse was imaginary.[20] I opened my eyes and could see the village now, growing in size as I approached. I watched through teary eyes as people; men and women, came racing out to watch me. I could see that they were doing something with their faces, but couldn't make out what. Maybe they were guessing my name? I waved and began singing the Irish national anthem with enthusiasm. Without warning, I was pushed to my left by something and my flight path started to alter. What was happening?! By Scud, they were blowing me off course!

'You vermin!' I yelled, 'I'm on a journey of peace!' But the fucks continued blowing; more and more of them joining in, and before long I sailed right past the village and on down towards the ground. I twisted my head around and looked back up at them as they watched me fall.

'You'll never pay for this!' I admitted with a scream and turned back around to look at my fate.

I was headed for a strange green patch on the ground which looked different from the surrounding rock. What is that? I thought as I lasered toward earth. In my last few seconds I tried to remember a prayer and failed. Then I hit the ground.

---

20. If Freud were reading that he'd interpret it as a secret longing for gorse! But joking aside, there may actually be some truth in that. I know Freud is talking about repressed desires in that regard, but I have always felt a sort of affinity with gorse. Not so much a desire for it, but a kind of closeness or bond. I know it might sound stupid, but sometimes when driving around gorse-heavy Wexford I feel ever-so-slightly safer. I'm not sure, but the gorse hallucination might have something to do with that?

But I didn't smash up like a human light bulb as I was expecting. Instead, a massive heap of congealed spit broke my fall. The years of people spitting over the edge had created a little mound of mucous, big enough to let me land alive, yet profoundly paralysed. I had seen into the village and that was all that mattered! As soon as I was released from the clinic I wrote this book, despite being paralysed from the lower eyelid down, by staring intently/ not intently at my mother.[21]

---

21. A collection of my satirical travel diaries, entitled *A Swift Amble About the Place*, (Belony, 2005). My urge to travel was inspired by the quote from legendary mythologist Joseph Cowbell: "A journey is a myth; it's the destination that is real."

# HAY THERE

It's amazing the things you can find under hay! I was out in my uncle's fields recently and came across a load of  mashed up carrots and parsnips under a partial bale! How did it get there?! I'm always finding mad shit under hay! In previous times I've found delft, a rotting dog, roof tiles, a purse, even the opening to some kind of citadel! There was some hay going in the entrance!

# GASP

I was looking under my bed for fun one day when I found a small hole in the floor. Curious as to why it was there, I made my way further under. My movement was restricted and I started to get panicky.

'This better be worth it!' I said aloud to the fluff, dusty coins and bit of Easter egg from long ago.[22] I put my hands by my side and wormed my way further along until my nose was hovering above the hole. The carpet was torn and frayed around the edges. I couldn't imagine what had caused it. There wasn't enough light to see properly so I dragged up one of my hands and stuck it deep into the hole. I immediately screamed out loud and yelled at my sister to stop pouring hot tea on my exposed foot.

'I'm sorry, I thought you were a drain!' she laughed and ran off down the stairs and out the front door. That was the last time I ever saw her.

---

22. Nothing better than a good Easter egg is there? Imagine the Creme Egg one's were full of goo!

# LIVER LET DIE

I lay on the operating table, almost sure the doctors didn't know I was actually awake.

'Don't cut me open yet!' I screamed in utter silence. 'I'm still awake!!' But none of the doctors paid any heed whatsoever. I gazed at them through my closed eyelids and hoped to God one of them was capable of receiving thoughts.

I was in hospital to have my liver removed. I had drank too much over the past six months and doctors decided that if I didn't have it replaced, I was going to die. I had little choice and was thrown onto the bottom of a long waiting list for a liver donation. I had done my best to rise to the top of it, having broken into the records room a few months previously to see who else was on the list.[23] After getting the names and addresses of the folk, I hunted down some of the children and killed them first as they were easier to get rid of. I chickened out however when it came to the adults and teens, afraid that they might fight back.[24]

I had only managed to pick off seven people out of twenty four ahead of me, and time was running out. In desperation I contacted a private hospital, hoping that I could maybe buy my life. But they told me their hands were tied and that all patients, private and public, worked

---

23. Fucking HSE. They got the list wrong TWICE. First by putting me on a list for delivering post around the wards and then by putting me on an internal shortlist to win "happiest patient under mortal circumstances." Eventually I was put on the correct liver donor list, but only after four Prime Time specials.
24. I did attempt to kill a lad who was about fifteen, but the person I had intended to frame for the murder was over at the Gaeltacht doing Irish college.

from the same donors list.

'But what if I was to bring in a liver I found on the curb??' I implored, imagining how easy it would be to pick off a homeless woman and 'borrow' her liver. But they replied in the negative.

'That is absurd. Maybe you need a brain transplant you desperately stupid fool.'

But I was unwilling to just drop it. After all, it was my life I was trying to save! Perhaps I had been simply talking to a particularly difficult individual who was having a bad day. I decided to try and bring in my own liver anyway.

Finding the person was easy but once they were dead and lying on my sofa, I found it difficult to figure out which part was actually the liver. I sliced out a few purpley looking organs and brought them down to the local vet to see if they could identify the liver.

'Oh hi vet, I just need to check which one of these is the liver - my cat is crazy about liver, the thing about liver is, the cat's crazy about it!!' I handed her over the slimy objects and she disposed of the bladder and stomach and put the liver into a handy bag for me.

'Cheers!' I said. 'The cat'll thank you!!' But it wasn't for the cat - it was for me, for a transplant I needed because I was going to die without one.[25]

I ran into Blackrock clinic and before I walked in the door, I threw the liver onto the path and kicked it around a little just so it looked more 'found.' I walked in the door and plopped the dry liver covered in dust on the counter.

'Eh I was talking to doctors the other day about getting this liver put into me for various reasons which I don't want to get into. I'm free now if you could get

---

25. I needed a liver for transplanting purposes.

someone for me.'

I was immediately rushed into surgery and the liver was put into some ice to cool it down. I lay on the table, trembling with terror about the pain I going to feel and wondering why the vet hadn't asked any more questions about why I had brought in a human liver to feed to my cat. This and other questions such as "did the doctors know I was actually awake?" circled around my brain, only fading when they began to saw into my head.

# SPACE QUERY

I found out recently that scientists are peering out into distant strata of space with highly advanced listening devices, hoping to catch an earful of alien intelligence. But what in quasar will constitute an intelligent sound?? What sort of sound are they looking for that they can separate from ordinary run of the mill universe sounds?[26] I wondered if maybe a pattern or some order would show that it was manufactured by beings, but apparently stars emit that sort of shit all the time. Puzzled I contacted NASA for some clarification. The conversation went as follows:

'Hi NASA? What are you listening for?'

'What do you mean sir?'

'What are you listening to in space?'

'I'm not sure I understand you sir.'

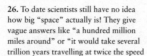

'What are you classing as alien sounds in space ye spook?'

'This is Greystones Garda station, what do you want?'

'You know what NASA are up to, patch me through now dick forest!'

'What is your name there?'

'It's 'Guns' no it's not, that's irrelevant - I want answers, what are you doing with my taxes up there in Hubble!! I demand answers now cocktail!!'

---

26. To date scientists still have no idea how big "space" actually is! They give vague answers like "a hundred million miles around" or "it would take several trillion years travelling at twice the speed of light to even reach the moon!" But they actually know very little about this sort of thing.

'You're going to get in serious trouble with this carry on'

'You'll never catch me space fag!'[27]

'I can see you right now outside the window on your mobile-'

With that I ran and was caught about 10 feet out to sea as I tried to swim to Wales. To this second I've still received no answers from those fascists.

---

27. The Garda was actually very upset that I called him a space fag. He mentioned his difficulty with the remark a number of times, explaining to me that a nephew of his was gay and had said the word space a good few times in the past.

# P.U.D.

I knew this lad called Pud about 12 year ago and he was a nightmare to bring to the amusements! The cunt was fascinated by lights and of course in an amusement place, what's there lot's of? Lights! He'd be there all looking at them and stuff all night and you'd think to yourself – Come on Pud! It's only lights!

# BRIBED LOGIC

Fuck wrapping presents. I'm so cool I cover the present in photos of the present so the person sees it before they open it! But it can cause problems, like what happened at my sister's birthday last February. The present I was giving her was a photo of the wrapping paper. But seeing as the wrapping paper was a photo of the present, when I gave it to her it sucked itself and a kitchen press into a fucked up black hole!

# I WOULD HAD
# I COULD HAVE

It was this day last year that I met myself on the bus. It was a miserable wet evening in the depths of November and I got on the bus, completely soaked. I was in a foul humour as I had just been kicked out of ballet for turning up to a second rehearsal naked. I paid the driver and slung my bag up onto the luggage slab. I looked for a seat and was greeted by a dozen sullen faces all staring out the condensation covered windows or sniffing and clearing their throats. I really didn't fancy sitting beside one of these horrors.[28]

I made my way upstairs and chose a seat near enough to the back on the right hand side. That way I could lay my head on the glass to my left, the way it felt most comfortable. The bus hummed on and I pointlessly had a peer out the window. All I could see beyond the reflection of the inside of the bus was a crystallised blur of headlights and traffic lights. I used my ticket to rub a larger viewing patch into the condensation, but it revealed little more. I took a quick look at the other people around me when something strange caught my eye. It was a person sitting a few seats in front on the other side. They looked exactly like me! This is so weird, I thought. I couldn't take my eyes off them. Curiosity got the better of me and I changed seats to be right behind them. My heart started to race. This person really did look identical to me.

---

28. Two things that wreck my head when I get on a bus, 1) When all the hot girls that get on sit downstairs and 2) the fact that no matter where I sit, a bottle ALWAYS rolls and comes to an excruciatingly irritating stop at my foot.

 'Sorry there's a fly going into your ear!' I said loudly to them. The person turned around and I received a jarring shock. It was me. No question about it. A moment of jelly-like insanity surged through my mind as I dealt with the meta-existential implications of seeing myself. I questioned for a moment whether I was maybe someone else going mad and only hallucinating that I was this person. I shot a look at my reflection in the window and was reassured that I was who I thought I was. But the situation still remained - it appeared this person was too! The doppelganger seemed completely unfazed by our similarity, casually asking if the fly was gone yet.

'Yes.. It.. It flew off downstairs,' I managed, the words feeling as awkward as gorse coming out of my mouth.

'Thanks', he replied and turned around. I sat speechless and conclusion-less. I reached forward and tapped the person on the shoulder.

'Is it back?' he asked.

'No' I replied, 'It's still downstairs.'

'Then what is it?'

'Don't you think we look remarkably similar?' I enquired.

'Yes,' he answered. 'We do.'

It was incredible to look at. I had seen myself in photographs, on video and in the mirror, but seeing myself in live 3D like this was unsettling. Everything about him was the same. Same haircut, same complexion, same eyes. That was the weirdest thing, the eyes. I felt like I couldn't look at them for longer than a second in case I totally lost touch with reason. I noted he had a slowly bleeding spot under his chin.

'Who are you?' I implored, frustrated with his nonchalance.

'Here, fuck off would you?' he said and got up and sat on a different seat.

I just sat there unable to do anything. My heart was still thundering in my chest and I was feeling close to panicking for some reason. It was like my anchors to the real world were being ripped up and I was afraid of drifting out to the misty depths of dementia.

Then I saw a girl with blond hair get on the bus and sit beside him. Her face was angelic and she had the grace of a porcelain fork. She was the sort of girl you could fall in love with after only a few minutes of staring. I watched as she leaned over, put her arm around my doppelganger and kissed him on the cheek.[29] He responded with a kiss to her mouth and they began tonguing intensely for a minute or two. When they were finished I saw him talk to her and then point in my direction. As she looked I blushed and then she started laughing out loud with a shrill, mocking voice. I caught her saying the words 'fucking ugly louse.' I've never felt so inadequate in my whole life. Even a girl who liked me didn't like me. My confidence valve was cut and masses of esteem cascaded out into the stuffy bus. I couldn't take any more. I got up and walked quickly to the stairs. I snatched a quick peek as I went down and saw them both mock waving at me. The last traces of esteem dribbled out my hole. I jumped off the bus and waited in the rain for another one.

I met myself just one other time after that upsetting

---

29. I remember distinctly that it was the cheek because I had a spot at the time where she kissed him (me) but I (him) did not. I'm assuming she would not have kissed him (me) if he (I) had a similar spot although I (me) can't say for certain.

occasion. I had been out at a dinner and was driving home late at night through the empty town when I came across a horrendous car wreck on the street. The car had smashed into the wall of a bank and was on fire.[30] I stopped the car and ran over to see if anyone was inside. I got a shock to see myself trapped inside, writhing in agony and looking at me with pleading eyes for assistance. I just stood with my mouth open. He was wrapped up in the seat belt and one of his legs was completely severed at the thigh by some crumpled metal. The stump bobbed up and down, vainly trying to give him some leverage to escape. The flames were attacking the windscreen fiercely and the searing heat was making his face begin to bubble. I looked at the door handle but was unable to do anything. I stood for a moment more before walking briskly back to my car, getting in and driving off at speed.

---

30. Earlier that day a friend had commented to me that banks were 'a source of unending misery for people.' I guess he was right!

# HALL OF DUST

My sister used to share a flat with this really weird guy called Ben. She was always telling me strange stories about him, but I found out for myself one Friday when I called over for dinner. Yer man was sitting on the sofa crying!

'Are you alright?' I asked him, but he just kept sobbing. I looked at my sister for explanation but she just beckoned me aside with a serious look on her face.

'Poor cunt's lost his key and it's killing him. I've tried cheering him up with Bond films, he loves them! But it's not working. Nothing is.'

I felt so sorry for him all of a sudden; this poor, pathetic, shrub of a man. I rolled up a fifty and popped it down his trousers to lift his spirits. He ignored it though, probably thought  I was teasing him with a pizza menu or something. After two more hours of crying we called an ambulance and he was taken away. His mother paid the rest of the rent and my sister replaced him with a girl called Panther.

# MYSTERIOUS NIGHT
# IN THE CELL

 It was a stormy mid October night and I was in the small local jail cell for robbing some vegetables from an old man's house. I lay up against the cold grimy bars, letting them hurt my cheek. I couldn't believe I had got caught. Sergeant Layte wouldn't let me out till morning which made me even angrier as I had left a CD on pause at home and couldn't stop thinking about it. The cell was one of four and was old and filthy. From where I stood I could see into the office and watched the sergeant swinging idly on his chair doing a Puzzler. Whether it was a Jig–word or a cryptic crossword was anyone's guess. I decided to go behind the sink for a sly wank when another policeman came bursting in the door.

'Sergeant Layte! There's been a murder!' he cried.

'Christ no!' replied the Sergeant. 'Who?!'

'I don't know Sarge!' said the man. 'We haven't caught anyone yet!'

'Not the murderer you cunt, who's been killed?!'

'Oh, sorry – Terence Baiste! The accountant with the ugly cat!'

'Jesus, how was he killed?' asked the Sergeant.

'He was strangled with a knife,' answered the man.

'What?! How?!' asked the Sergeant incredulously.

'No one knows, but it gets stranger – his digital

camera was found beside his body and there was a picture of him and Randall McQuaid standing hand in hand!'

'So?' asked the Sergeant, confused.

'Sarge – Randall McQuaid died 2 years ago today, he was killed by a box!'

'No he wasn't, look he's outside the window bouncing a ball – where did you hear that??!' asked the Sergeant, losing patience.

'It was in the newspaper, look.' The man handed Sergeant Layte a newspaper.

'This says Randall McQuaid lied in a boxing match two years ago! What's wrong with you?!' shouted the sergeant.

'Aw come on Sarge, you know I've got no eyes,' answered the officer timidly.

'Yeah well get some surgery or something,' said the Sergeant. Just then there was another bustle at the door. Another cop crashed in and announced: 'Sergeant – we know who the murderer is!'[13]

But I had lost interest at this stage and slid quietly behind the sink while they were distracted.

---

31. I found out afterwards that the murderer was from a place called Lowicz in Poland. The same place my friend Thomas lost his iPod in 2006. Sometimes coincidence is a little too freaky!!!

# REASONABLY UNTITLED

I remember seeing a man dancing around the housing estates where I grew up as a child. They called him The Snowflake because of his graceful moves, but in reality he was not made of snow. He had a set route that he stuck to daily, dancing non-stop along it. He would appear every day in my estate around eleven in the morning and passed right by my house. Thinking back about him now always reminds me of being sick off school, because that was really the only time you ever saw him. He was never there during the summer. If I was home from school, I'd sit by the net curtains in my sitting room waiting with refined anticipation for the scraping of his shoes on the path. As soon as I'd hear it, I'd sweep the net curtains aside and peer out with all my might. Within seconds The Snowflake would dance gaily past, a shuffling portrait of utter merriment and I'd clap my hands with glee.

His appearance changed little over the years. He always wore a faded denim shirt, tucked into faded denim jeans with a massive bunch of keys jangling at his side. He had slicked back silver hair and a purple/red face.

One day, as suddenly as he appeared he disappeared. He simply stopped dancing through the estates. Some say he tripped over someone's bin and was beaten to death, some say he danced off into the sky and others insist he

went to jail. Who knows if any of these are true. All I
know is that net curtains + dancing man = divine youth.

# BLACK DEMISE

I was on my way to a distant planet when I discovered I couldn't breathe because I was standing outside my ship taking a piss. Gasping for oxygen but only inhaling a toxic mix of helium and hydrogen I began to panic. How could I have left the safety of the craft without my suit on??! I'm such a planet-prick!!! With only seconds of life left I tried desperately to scramble back into the cockpit. As I did I could see my wife staring at me with cold, evil eyes. She waved her hand at me in a slow deliberate motion and pressed a button causing the ship to zip off into the distance, leaving me spinning in black nothingness. My lungs felt like they were about to burst. I reached into my pocket and pulled out a pen and piece of space paper and wrote down my last actions. I've just realised I probably have another ten seconds or so, I thought I wouldn't even last this long. In saying that the pain I'm feeling in my chest right now is incomparable! Panic is literally exploding throughout my body and my relentless gasps for oxygen are proving useless. I am going to die any moment now and I will find out whether there is life after living or not! My god, the electric pain and pressure inside my head is unreal! I can barely write!! Oh shit, I think I'm beginning to lose concsoiness.. I can thin straight. I wondr wher I going to now thtf it ll fade like a suuun un ij homo fuf fuf fuf fuf fuff

# THE PAINTING

I walked into the painting, utterly shocked that I could do so at all. And I literally mean into the painting. I was in the National Gallery on Breathe Street when I came across the piece. I had been without friends for some time and the gallery allowed me space to gloat upon my feelings of wretchery. The painting was hanging at the end of a long corridor and it stretched almost from the floor to the ceiling. It was an oil painting, depicting a quaint little cottage in a cosy forest clearing. Smoke curled lazily from the chimney and a neat stack of logs sat by the front door. It was a scene of the serene and I realised then that it was paradise for me. I knew, objectively, that it would be my final resting place. I needed to find out where this cottage was and go there. I looked at the gold plate beneath it:

*The Painting by Hans Lung 1659-?*

I had to find out more about this man and where this magical place he had painted was located. I knew in my heart and soul that it still existed. That it had not been turned into an Estate Agent's or a Cul De Sac. I spent the next hour breathing in the remarkable image, savouring the depth of fulfilment it gave me. I allowed my senses to embark on a journey of cerebral wonder through the painting's charms, imagining all sorts of things I would do if I arrived there. As I admired it I unconsciously crept gradually closer. Soon I realised I was nearly touching up against it, barely an electron away. That's when I felt the sudden urge to walk right into it. I took a quick glance behind me, saw no one was there and walked forwards.

It literally just felt like I was walking off a bus or something. Just going from inside to out. I was simply now in the painting. My view of the scene was obscured; I could see nothing more than what I could see from standing outside looking in. Everything around me just ended in imminent horizons; above, below, left and right. The perspective was unnatural to me; it felt almost like an optical illusion or a trick of the eye, or a trick of the light and the eye. Everything was very clearly made of paint, but in an indescribable 3D but at the same time not 3D way.

5D?

3D/2D?

The cottage stood in front of me and it was very much paint too. It was beautiful. I stared for an indefinite amount of time at the dark, static trees above it. They understood something I could never grasp. Maybe something from my previous life. Maybe I'd never know, or maybe some answers might lie in the cottage. I tried to walk towards it but it was about as useful as a thumb-tack the size of the sun. My attempt at movement felt like I was on an invisible treadmill; a distant sensation of moving, but no real change in my perspective. I was never any closer to the cottage. I bent down to touch the ground, but my hand never actually connected with it. It was then I noticed that my hand was paint too. It was like I was a breath of air diffused inside some more air. I wanted to turn around and go back but there was no turning around. My only possible view was of the painting. It took in my whole perspective. Oh well, I thought. Better get used to paint.

# THE SLOTS PART I

I was in a local amusement arcade recently when I thought it was high time to win some money on the slot machines. They were in the second half of the building so I had to go through the rest of the fun machines to get to them. My capacity to ignore these icons of amusement was nil existent, so before I could reach the slots I was standing in front of a brightly lit claw machine, staring at its enticing guts.

There were some five and ten euro notes and a couple of expensive looking watches on offer. It was two euro to play so I guessed it was worth the gamble. I fed in the money and grabbed the joy and buttons. The claw shuddered into life and glided across to the potential booty. I skilfully lowered it to a watch and pressed the grab button.

'Yes!!' I hissed as it caught the watch by the strap. It started to ascend and then wobbled over towards the exit chute. Just as it reached the end it wobbled a little more but dropped the prize perfectly down the chute into my hands.

'Yay!' I shouted with joy and put it on straight away. I swanned over to the entrance to the slot machines and made a stop at the change cage.

'Could I have a flower pot with twenty euro of coin in it?!' I asked happily.

'Of course! Just make sure you give me the twenty euro first!!!' replied the lady and released a scream of laughter which caused her to drop her éclair.

'Oh the intention's all mine!' I replied wittily and quickly folded the twenty into a little airplane and threw it skilfully into the cage. She blushed and gave me a pot full of coins. Utterly pleased with myself I walked on into the slot area.

It was dark and filled with the mysterious analogue sound of the slots. The room was mainly populated by older ladies and the place reminded me of some sort of Joycian forest.[32] I wandered through, watching as the pros pulled the levers and pressed the buttons like Eskimos who had been transformed into old women. They were all desperately serious, the only ones showing any emotions at all being the winners, who would scream and punch the air repeatedly in the moments after triumph.

I was trying to pick a suitable machine and eventually decided on one over in a hidden corner. It looked older than and not as used as the rest of them. This is as good as any, I supposed and started to fill it with coins. My luck from the claw game didn't seem to be following me to this machine. I was about to walk away from it when a diamond fell out of my pocket. It landed on the ornate carpet and rolled behind the machine. Shit, better get that, I thought and got down on my hands and knees to retrieve it. As I looked behind the machine I realised that there was some sort of portal to another world there. My diamond! It's gone into a different dimension or

---

32. Known as "the ladies of the lights" in Bray, a town near to where I live. Sexual deviants can be seen hanging around outside slot houses hoping to catch a glimpse of these divine beauties stepping out for a fag or two.

something! I have to get it back, it's worth nearly a million euro! I didn't know what to do. Should I contact scientists and let the world know about this bizarre phenomenon? Or should I get my diamond first and then tell everyone about the mysterious portal? I made my decision and was about to execute it when I received a text on my phone. It was my mother. She wanted to know which potato I wanted for dinner; Records or Roosters.

'Not now Mother, I'm busy,' I replied and crawled towards the portal...

# THE SLOTS PART 2

But it turned out it wasn't a portal to a different world, someone had just left a lighting nightlight behind the machine. I ran home and tucked into my spuds with relish.

# THE SLOTS PART 3 - THE HOMECOMING

The spuds turned out to be Kerr's Pink!

# ADELAIDE STREET

I was walking down the road the other day  whistling the theme tune to ER when I heard a woman laughing into her mobile.

'I love to kill cock!' she announced, spraying the place with a smile. Disgusted and appalled, I jumped to malekind's defence.

'Who by fuck do you think you are?!' I shouted. 'You feminists are all so similar! How would you like it if I doused your breasts in paraffin and set them alight? Would you still be thinking of a mountain of dead dicks then?! Or what if I took your Mars Delight? How would you even cope for the rest of the day?! You're nothing short of slug dung Madame.'

The woman regarded me with horror. Suddenly I noticed the t-shirt she was wearing. Printed across the front was - 'I live in Kilcock.'[33]

---

33. Worth noting that the font on the t-shirt is identical to a font on the wall of the Mermaid Theatre in Bray. In the Mermaid's Betelnut café there is a sign on the wall saying 'theatre.' This is the font I refer to.

# IRISH SECRET SERVICE

I didn't even know an Irish secret service existed up until 2 weeks ago when I tried to download a bomb from Indymedia. I accidentally stumbled onto their page describing the structure of the military intelligence service, more commonly know as G2.

Intrigued, I tried to find out more about this clandestine operation, so I rang up my friend, Garda Pat Gumm.

'Pat, howya? Do you know anything about the secret service here in Eire??' I asked.

'Jaysus, do you mean the lads in Special Branch, they're a shower of pricks - don't piss them off whatever you do!!' he replied.

'Come on, you know I wouldn't do a thing like that Pat!! Hahahahahahahahahahahahahahaha!!!! I'm talking more specifically about G2, the military secret service - have you ever dealt with those cunts?'

There was silence apart from the sound of Pat chewing loudly on what sounded like crisps.

'Pat?' I asked

'Hmmm. G2... The lads that do be meeting up with the top brass here about ministers and terrorists and spies and stuff?'

'I suppose so,' I answered. 'Tell me everything about them, I'm fascinated!'

'Well I hope you haven't gotten into any trouble with

them, if you think Special Branch are dickheads, these guys are dickheads multiplied by a hundred thousand million!!' said Pat.

'A hundred billion?!' I exclaimed.

'Oh yes,' said Pat. 'Nasty work, but absolutely vital to the country. They were instrumental in stopping some lads burning down An Taoiseach's hedge last year, then they arrested a chap from Iceland in Dublin Airport last March on suspicion of terrorism. Think about it, why fly from Iceland?'

'I suppose so,' I said my voice vibrating with wonder. 'How in fuck do you join, do you have to be a soldier first?'

'Not sure,' he replied. 'I'll ask Bunty if there's any jobs going now. There's a training course in some place down the country where you learn how to spy and that sort of thing, I hear it's very good. I wouldn't be on for that myself though, I prefer being Deputy Commissioner! Listen I have to go, I'll get you an application form anyway and pass it across to them and see what they say! Have a good one!!'

'Nice one Pat!! Thanks a hundred thousand million!'

'Ahahahahahahahahahaha!!! See ya good luck!' he said and hung up.

As I walked away from the telephone, I can't be sure, but I'm almost positive I saw someone running away from my house in camo and jumping upside down into the back of a red sports car which tore away instantly. They're good, I thought, they're good, and started to put on some clothes.

# PURPLE GLUON

My mate was pissed one night and told us he'd
eat a pint of paint flakes for a hundred euro.

'Bollox!' we called. 'Rumpole!' But he
was serious. Two minutes later a pint glass
full of white paint flakes off an old door in the
shed was sitting in front of him. Laughs bounced around the
room as tenners and fivers materialised on the kitchen table.
As soon as it reached one hundred my mate picked up the
glass and started to pour the dry shavings into his mouth.
I watched as he chewed and swallowed lumps of spit and
flake. All I could imagine was the taste after biting a pencil
for ages. Half way through he ran into difficulty and paused
for a moment, trying to cough up some shards that were
clinging to the back of his throat. He tipped the glass to his
lips again and allowed more flakes to slide into his gob. This
time he accidentally breathed some into his lungs sending
him into a painful coughing fit. He gave up and spent the
rest of the night coughing, hacking and retching.[34]

---

34. This guy was always doing stupid
stuff. Last time I saw him he was pinned
down in Centra on Dame St by a load
of security guards. He was wearing
matching white denim jeans and jacket
and was surrounded by porn magazines
he had obviously attempted to rob.

# NOTHING'S SACREDD

'Fine bollix on tha' one!'

'Couldn't a said it better meself Rover.'

'Here d'ya ever wonder if maybe our world isn't the way we think it is? That all sorts of infinite possibilities exist but we can't recognize them because we're imprisoned by our five senses?'

'Not a chance ye cunt!'

\* \* \*

'Get back to work ya gumpty fucks!'

# SEAING STARS

A man sat on a rock at the edge of the sea. The view was beautiful. Bright sunlight reflected off the waves off into the distance and a cool breeze helped shore up the pleasant atmosphere. Everything about the setting was soothing. The sound of the surf crashing softly against the rocks, the smell of summer on the air and the heat of the sun on his back. The man gazed steadily out at the horizon, trying to see as far as he could. A pipe with some smouldering tobacco, hung idly from his mouth.

'A time for relaxation. No?' he asked a crab skeleton in a rough but gentle voice. The skeleton was as mute as a thumb.

'Ah, don't want to answer then, eh?' he asked again, this time crushing the crab with his pipe. It had been dead two days so no gods frowned. A starfish walked up a rock, its body glistening in the sun. It made its way up to the man and sat beside him. They sat in silence for a few moments. Maybe the man hadn't noticed the small invertebrate arriving, but after a short while the starfish spoke.

'Hello sir, I've a question. Why do you stare mildly out to ocean?'

'Oh hi starfish, I'm sorry, I didn't notice you arrive! Are you well? I'm well. Now to answer your question! I stare out to ocean because I need to think and the ocean calms my mind. I was at Mrs Dawkins's house up the beach this morning. She's a quaint old bitch and I do work for her, sanding her blue boat which she keeps out the front. I was working away when I felt the urge for some tea. I walked into her cottage and into the kitchen where she was painting an image. I asked her if I could make a cup of tea. "No you can't you slug, get back to that boat now and finish the job!! Finish a job!" she yelled. In a momentary fit of rage I stormed out, calling her a hag made of dog's balls. Now I'm afraid word may get out around the village about this and I'll never get a boat-sanding job again! I've come here to try and figure this mess out.'

The starfish shook its head (one of its legs). 'Wow that is a bit of a mess. But at the same time Mrs. Dawkins sounds quite mean. Having a job is important, but you also deserve to be treated with respect! I'd send her a fax apologising for using the words "hag" and "balls", but explain that you believe her behaviour was out of line. If the villagers hear of the incident, you can defend your honour by telling them you reacted in passion, but have since apologised! Too many boats need sanding around here for people to care very much about a few cross words with Mrs. Dawkins!'

The man was very impressed. 'Such logic and psychological understanding for a sea insect!' he cried. 'You truly are a gallon of help! I will try your plan, I hope it works!'

'I hope it does too,' replied the starfish. With that the man stood up and ran to buy a fax machine.

# EMERGENCY!

'Oh hi!' I shout over to my friend, but he just looks at me like I'm a bag of spare bolts.

'Liver, it's me Foke!' I try, but again his eyes sit on me with all the recognition of a couple of tits. This isn't like him, I think to myself. Maybe he's in a coma. I run over and push a fork into his eye and he screams but then resumes his state of bloated indifference.

'Liver!!' I shout right in his face, but the only reaction is his hair swaying softly on my breath. I slip my phone out of my phone pocket and launch a couple of numbers at it: 9-9-9. I place the dots of the earbit up to my lobe and listen, all the while, *all the while* keeping both eyes pasted to my quasi-zombied colleague.

'Emergency services what service do you require?' comes a small electronic copy of someone's voice out of the phone.

'Ambulance, psychiatrists - both!' I reply, a little panicked. 'My friend's in a trance'

'Hold on one moment,' they say and I'm transferred.

'Ambulance, what's your location?' comes a new voice. I give him my where and go on to explain the situation.

'My friend's in some sort of zombie-like trance. He can feel pain but he doesn't even know who I am!!'

'Right, stay on the line, we are sending an ambulance out to you right now, has he taken any drugs or alcohol or medication?' asks the phone.

'Of course not!!' I cry. 'He's ninety years old!!' I sever the call in fury and look at my friend again. But now that the clouds have passed I realize in the sunlight that I don't even know this person, let alone where I am. God knows where I sent that ambulance. I squint and move my head to within an inch of this person's face. No, I certainly don't know this man. Luckily he doesn't seem to know what's going on. I tip-toe slowly away and run to a nearby chipper only leaving when they call the police.

# ZZZZ

I have this recurring dream that I'm waking up from a dream. Now it's hard to tell sometimes if I'm waking up or whether I'm just dreaming I am. Sometimes I dream I'm  actually waking up, sometimes I dream I'm only dreaming I'm waking up and sometimes I dream I'm just dreaming and don't wake up. Pissed off and confused, I put a video camera above me to see if I could work it all out. When I bounced awake (literally!) I ran over and hooked up my camera to my TV. On the footage I saw one of my posters falling down at some point in the middle of the night and little else.

# DESPERATE MEANS AND TRAGIC SCENES

If this message finds you, I need help. Immediately. I am trapped in a room and I don't know where it is. I'm being held captive. I was watching a film in the cinema one moment and the next I'm tied up in the back of a van, being driven here. Where here is is a mystery to me though. It may or may not even be in Dublin, I don't know how far I've been taken. I was blindfolded and led up stairs to this room. It's bare; white walls and nothing in it. There's an empty drawer on the ground to poo and piss in and it's emptied at the end of every day by gloved hands which come through a little hatch at the door. Food and water comes in through the same hatch, three times a day. Mostly spuds. I do have a companion here, my Mum's best friend, Maureen Delaney.[35] She is just as clueless as me. It's awkward, we have nothing in common. I fear she may try to develop a relationship or something. I am in trouble, if you're reading this, please come  and help me. Look for me, I need to get out. No time for writing my name or any other details. Get the police, tell them everything that's happened and then look for me. I know that the building is not near a railway because I've heard no trains. May the Lord cast a die in my favour. Thank you.

---

35. No word of a lie here, but she looks *exactly* like the lady aged 54 in Bartholomeus van der Helst's "Portrait of an Old Lady, Aged 54", which currently resides in the National Gallery of Ireland. If you want to have a look for yourself it is situated in room 38 of the Milltown wing. The room has a keenly decorated wooden frame and a smoke alarm with a red dot on it in the centre of the ceiling.

# TIED DOWN

I can't feel my head. I can't see either, but more importantly than that I can't feel my head. I'm lying down, I know that much and I'm not in any great pain, but it feels like there's a stone where my head should be. If my head's gone, how am

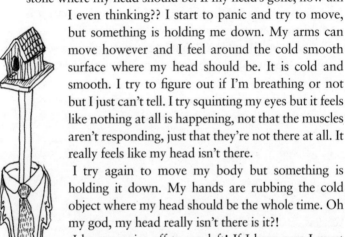

I even thinking?? I start to panic and try to move, but something is holding me down. My arms can move however and I feel around the cold smooth surface where my head should be. It is cold and smooth. I try to figure out if I'm breathing or not but I just can't tell. I try squinting my eyes but it feels like nothing at all is happening, not that the muscles aren't responding, just that they're not there at all. It really feels like my head isn't there.

I try again to move my body but something is holding it down. My hands are rubbing the cold object where my head should be the whole time. Oh my god, my head really isn't there is it?!

I hear a noise off to my left! If I have ears I must have a head, I reason. I try to shout something but again there is just nothing where my mouth should be. No sound, nothing. That noise sounds like a heavy iron gate opening. There is a loud squeak of metal and then a clang as the door or whatever it is, is shut.

'Are you awake?' asks a voice. I wave my arm and open and close my fist wildly in reply.

'Good,' says the voice. 'You were involved in a surgical mishap. Did you do anything to annoy the doctors?' I flatten my hand and swing it from side to side in a definite 'no'.

'Well someone did because they have stuck a stone onto your neck and thrown your head out into the woods!' says the voice. I try to take it all in.

'Out in the woods! No place for a head!' continues the voice. 'You're probably wondering why you can hear me. Well the answer is simple, they've sewn your ear onto your chest! The woods is no place for a head but I'm afraid it will have to stay there because I have no idea where exactly it is and those grumpy medical chaps will not tell me!'

Gobdaws, I say in my mind and try to make a sound similar to the word by rubbing my hand off my side, but I fail.

'Goodnight,' says the voice and I hear the gate open and close again. I fall asleep with my hands on my stone.

# PERFUME

A few weeks ago I decided to go into Brown
Thomas to look for some male perfume as I
was feeling very lonely. I entered the bustling
building and was immediately doused with the
smell of cosmetics and outrageous spending habits. I looked
around at the various counters and approached a girl for
some assistance. I looked for her eyes among her make-up
and enquired as to where would be the best place to look for
a fragrance that would attract women.

'In a bin!' she replied with a gale of laughter. 'Ah no
I'm only joking, over there at the Hugo Boss counter there's
loads of shit for men to splash on.' I thanked her and asked
if she'd like to go to out for a meal after work. She puked a
little onto her sleeve and told me to fuck off and stop eating
into her commission time. I walked away, a little angered,
towards the wall of male perfumes.

A man with carefully blended hair stood beside me
and I watched to see how he chose his scent. He picked out
a Versace bottle shaped like a testicle and sprayed a small
amount onto his wrist. After a moment he sniffed it and took
one. I waited till he walked away and took the tester and
sprayed my wrist. The smell reminded me of my rich uncle.
A sweet, demanding fragrance. Convinced this would leave
girls with little or no option but to find me sensitive, caring
and worthy of their time I brought a few bottles into the

jacks. I had no intention of paying for this stuff, after all I did have a right to be loved.[36] I also had not owned any money for a considerable amount of time. Once inside the posh cubicle I emptied the glass testicles into a 2 litre Coke bottle I had in my bag. I then got rid of the empties by smashing them on the ground and putting the glass fragments into the toilet via tissue. As I walked out of the toilet I was grabbed by two security guards. I wrenched myself free and poured the perfume over myself.

'You'll never take me alive!' I screamed and lit my soaked clothes with a lighter. I suffered moderate burns to my neck and ear and must thank the security guards for putting me out before I did more severe damage to myself. Lesson? Use Lynx - all perfume does is attract trouble!!!! Ahahahaha if only 'Eyed' known!

---

36. This wasn't the first time I had used this toilet to rob stuff. A good few months previously I had stolen some crystal figurines and very nearly got caught. I used the same trick of bringing them to the toilets and hiding them in my bag. But I was too cocky. Even before I got to the front door I thought it would be ok to take them out of my bag again to admire them. Big mistake. A security guard standing less than two feet away saw me taking them out of the bag and asked me if I had a receipt. In panic I just bolted out the door. The guard chased hot on my heels as I ran across Wicklow Street and into a pissy alley. Luckily for me the security guard was too disgusted to follow.

# SAD SOUP

I was walking out of the doctor's the other day when I saw a man over ten feet tall walking down Rathmine main street. He was a strange looking gentleman and not exclusively as a result of his tall standing. He also had no ears or nose. Instead of a nose he had a narrow, rubbery tube about the size of a drinking straw which dangled down about two feet or so. Every now and then he'd toss it over his shoulder out of his way like an unwanted fringe, but it would always fall back to dangle in front of his chest. In the place of ears he had small skin grills at the sides of his head. He was wearing a fine looking suit which he must have had tailored specifically for him because of his size and I estimated it would have cost a smart bank note or two. I decided to follow this fascinating giant to see where he would go.

The sunny street was busy with lunchtime workers racing about but he made his way easily through them. Nobody seemed to want to touch this big cunt. He never looked from side to side, staring straight ahead as he lumbered along. I took out my mobile and pretended to talk to a vet so that I would blend into the background.

After a minute or so, he stepped off the curb and crossed the street. I followed and watched as a car smashed into his legs, causing him to slam violently off the bonnet and windscreen. I stopped dead in my tracks and suddenly felt myself lurching sideways as a car slammed into my own

hip. Explosive pain splashed across my
entire body as I was hurled onto the road.
I smacked the tarmac with a loud slap
and lay in a lake of agony. I strained to
look over at the giant and could see him
lying motionless on the road, a puddle of
blood the size of a page splashed beside his head. A crowd
of people were gathered around him and within moments he
had caught fire.

Someone grabbed me off the road and I was roughly
thrown onto the curb. I couldn't move with the pain. The
giant was covered in flames now and the traffic started to
move again and people resumed their busy rushing about. I
watched helplessly as the giant turned from a raging torch
into a smouldering lump, sparks exploding every time a tyre
hit off him. After a few hours I regained enough strength
to crawl back into the doctor and have my shattered hip
amputated. As the warming painkillers flooded through
my system I wondered what the giant's name had been. It
wouldn't have surprised me if he didn't have one at all.

# TWO CLIFFS

If I was to try to jump across two massive cliff faces towering over a colossal ravine what would you think? Before you answer, I want you to picture my attempt first. I'm standing on the dusty edge taking a quick look before I jump. I can see the other cliff edge off in the distance. The wind blows softly on my face, I think for a moment I can smell cat food, but it couldn't be. How many steps do I need? Four? Eighteen? Any more and I'll be too tired to jump by the time I get to the edge. I walk back eighteen paces and start to run towards the edge. I panic a little bit as it comes racing towards me but it's too late so I just leap into the air with all my might. Now whether I make it or not depends on a few things. Was I molested as a youth? Do I suffer from any life-affecting mental disorders? Have I ever witnessed my dog accidentally being run over by my dad? Have I ever watched an 18's film before I was 18???[37] One thing's for certain – Life is a lot more powerful than gravity.

---

37. The earliest 18's film I can recall watching was Robocop. I was traumatised by the bit where the goblin came out of the woods and starts shooting Robocop. But it's great then when Robocop cuts him in half. 'This is the law!' I'll never forget it!!

# STUCK IN THE LIFT

Hands up who hates getting stuck in lifts?

"Me!!"

Yeah, me too - it's horrendous. A month ago I was spending some time in Clery's department shop when I decided to get the elevator up to the potz 'n' panz section on the fifth floor. I loved to look around at the shiny displays of stainless steel and quizz workers on the prices of knives. I waited at the doors of the ground floor lift for a few moments, waiting for the doors to open. An attractive girl with blonde hair stood beside me. I offered her a bite of my Iceberger but she politely refused.

'Not really the weather for them is it?!' I joked cheerfully. The doors opened and I let an elderly couple out before stepping in. The girl entered as well.

'Where you off to? Space?!' I asked, on a fiery humourous roll. ''Cause I don't think it goes that far!'

She smiled a little. 'No, just the fifth floor.'[38]

'Pots?' I asked enthusiastically.

'No,' She replied. 'The bathroom.'

'Haha, we do have a pot to piss in up there!' I laughed and punched the fifth floor button. The elevator lurched against gravity and I felt a pleasing tug at my innards as we rose through the shaft.

'Always reminds me of Die Hard!' I told her. 'Except do you ever notice that lifts never seem to have those exit

---

38. Apparently I was mistaken – I recently discovered that Clery's in fact only has three stories! A morsel of knowledge provided by my Uncle Ray who was in there today buying some stuff.

hatches they always have in the flicks!'

'Yeah,' she replied, probably trying to stifle a giggle. The elevator continued to rise past the third floor when it suddenly shuddered to a halt.

'Driver, what's the meaning of this!' I joked. I wanted to remain calm and humourous so as not to upset the girl. I knew how women get in situations like these. I punched the number 5 button again, quite hard so there was no mistaking that was the floor I wanted.

'Just leave it,' said the girl. 'You might break it.' I have to say this put me out a little, after all I had been nothing but nice to her all along.

'Shut the fuck up before I eat you,' I spat at her. 'I'm only trying to help.' She regarded me with worried eyes and took out her mobile phone.

'No need for that!' I said, smacking it out of her hand. 'We're perfectly safe, no need for those sorts of things!' She immediately started to call for help. I rolled my fists in anger. What a bitch! A muffled voice responded after two or three calls.

'Hi there, don't panic. There's a temporary fault with the lift. You're in absolutely no danger, there's an engineer fixing the problem right now, you'll be out in a minute or two.'

I started to panic. What if the engineer fell asleep and never completed the job?! What if we were stuck in the lift for months?! I decided to take extreme action. I grabbed the girl by the throat and yelled at the voice.

'I've got a fucking hostage in here! Get me the fuck out of here before I fucking murder her! I fucking mean it!! Clery's will be sorry!" The girl started whimpering and shaking with fear.

'Shhh!' I said smiling. 'It'll get us out quicker! I know what I'm do-' But before I finished the sentence the lift jolted into life again and the doors opened a moment later. I let go of her neck and was overpowered immediately by five or six men.

'What's wrong with you?!' one shouted into my ear.

'I'm just so terribly lonely,' I replied.

# AN ICY LUCK

It's snowing. I open my eyes and feel an icy flake land and melt on my lip. Where the craic am I? I think as I take in the view in front of me. The light is dim and I can see trees stretching into darkness. Snow covers everything and there is a dark, silent pressure pushing down. I scan my mind to try and remember what I'm doing here but I'm met with a curtain of amnesia. The last memory I can recall is a day with my family where I lost my holiday savings in a 20p-coin-pushing amusement machine. Feeling even more hard done by I stand up and take a panoramic look around. I'm greeted by the same view everywhere; a dark and silent snowy woods. The cold is sharp. I slip my hands in my pockets and start to walk in a random direction, trying desperately to figure out how I got here. After ten minutes of trudging through the snow I'm still no closer to an understanding. The view remains identical and I start to worry I may succumb to hypothermia which would cause my enzymes to become denatured, make chemical reactions impossible and eventually lead to my death. I press on, finding a pack of KP peanuts in my pocket and snack on them hungrily.

After about an hour I see what looks like a light in the distance. Probably a mirage, I think and turn back the way I came and start retracing my steps to where I started from.

My hands, feet and face are completely numb and the light breeze seems to cut right through my t-shirt. Wherever

I was before now, I certainly wasn't dressed for winter!! As I'm walking, the snow starts to fall heavier and I am no closer to finding any signs of life or an answer as to why I'm here. I begin to contemplate strange ideas like whether I'm in Narnia somehow or in a Truman Showesque reality TV programme where they dump unwitting people into strange situations to see how they cope. 'God it's real cold! I'll probably die in a minute or two, I hope I get rescued shortly!' I say loudly in case it is a television show. But no producers come running out of the darkness with blankets or assistants with cups of coffee. As soon as the thought of coffee hits me I realise I need to pee and poo quite urgently. I urinate into a mound of snow, letting the steam caress my face, enjoying its warmth. I then pull down my tracksuit bottoms and push out a shit with relative ease. With no leaves around I'm forced to wipe with some snow. I stare at the steaming poo for a few minutes with wide, tired eyes, my strength truly sapped. I may die soon, I think and continue on.

After another hour it becomes clear I am totally lost and have no idea where my starting point is. I keep walking, feeling like I might collapse at any given moment. My 'just keep goings' have run out, it's up to fate where I fall now. The trees start to thin out a little and I see that I've come to the edge of a small frozen lake. It is surrounded on all sides by powdery white trees. The surface is completely still and there is a seemingly reverent hush in the air. I feebly make my way over to it and notice that some of it is not covered by ice. I look into the water and see what looks like a telephone. This is my only chance, I think and dive in. The water is not so much hot as agonisingly ice cold. I feel like a trillion penknives are cutting into me as I flail about in the water trying to reach the phone. I manage to grab it and pull my self out, shivering violently. I look closer at the phone. I find the on button and press it, hoping it will work. My whole body is convulsing and I find it difficult to even breathe. Nothing happens, so I press it again. This time a welcome screen pops up and I scream with joy. I type in the European emergency code and am transported straight through to an operator.

'Hold on!' they say. 'We're coming to get you via GPRS!'

I let my head fall in the snow and cry with happiness. When they finally get to me a wolf has taken most of my left leg, but it was frozen anyway so I barely felt it.

'Maybe you'll be starting a new line of human flavoured ice pops!' laughs a paramedic.

'No,' I reply. 'The thought disgusts me.'

# R.O.B.O.T.

Anyone could be a robot. How do you know your dog isn't a robot? Or your doctor? Or that guy who fell over spilling wires out of his abdomen onto the street? How about YOU. Do you see #//~01001011+~^^@\|> instead of letters when you read this? Do you eat porridge or bolts? The brain is a muscle. Or is it??

# DINNER AT MY FRIEND'S

It was a disaster. We all fell ill after a few hours and made our way into the sitting room to get a little more comfortable. All of us, lying on chairs and the sofa, all of us in gastric pain. Przeck was the first to burst. He simply popped like a zit. One second he was there on the armchair, the next he was an assortment of organs on the carpet, curtains and mantelpiece. Everyone was too tired and sore to react. We all looked at each other knowingly, but no one said anything. A moment later, Frieda's head popped and her body rolled off the sofa onto the rug in front of the fire. I swear to God, one of her eyes landed in the keyhole of the door! I couldn't believe it, now two of my friends were gone. Would I be next? I tried with all my might not to burst, but I could feel my insides shifting about like a fork truck in a little yard. I remember then that Kurwa got up to stoke the fire or something and exploded right into it! Putting the yoke out entirely! That raised a little smile on my lips and on Gilda's lips too. Except as soon as she smiled, her whole body erupted through her mouth. The most impressive vomit ever - herself!

It was at least another three hours before I could even get up. Thank fuck I didn't burst too.

# UP SLACK

I was leaving my house to go to work one morning only to find someone had built a wall in front of my porch completely blocking me from going out the front door. The back door was impossible to open and anyway there was a lion in my back garden which I was sure would savage me if I tried to walk past it. All the windows were made of bullet proof glass and didn't open and the chimney was packed with wool. I essentially had no means of escaping my house!

I was about to contact the police when I remembered that I had left the phone under the grill all night and it was aft but a melted slab of plastic goop. I walked into the sitting room and sat down on the sofa to think about how I could get out. I know! I thought, I can smoke myself out! If I light a fire in the fireplace, all the smoke will pour out into the room coz the chimney's full of wool!

I ran to the 'place and ripped open a carton of zip and threw in some coals, whistling cheerfully at the possibility of imminent escape. I had to be careful with the flames so that the wool in the 'ney didn't catch, so as soon as the fire was going well I started to cover it with one of my favourite substances ever - slack. I slopped the glistening black fuel into the fire and winked at the mantelpiece as smoke began to fill the room. Soon breathing became difficult and my vision and my eyes were painfully hard to open. I began to realise that there was a flaw somewhere in my plan and the escape was not happening as intended. I also noticed the wool had caught fire despite my best efforts. I stumbled out of the sitting room and upstairs to the landing where there was less smoke. It was still very uncomfortable so I climbed up into my attic and crawled to a corner where the roof sloped down completely to the attic floor.

'Help!!!!' I screamed through a tiny hole about the size of a Malteser.

'Help!!!!' I continued screaming for my life. After 45 minutes my neighbour Dazzy smashed down the porch wall in his JCB and rescued me.[39]

---

39. Dazzy's a great chap. Obsessed with floods though. He has hundreds of documentaries recorded off the TV about floods and has even flooded his own house about fourteen times!

# THE KNOWLEDGE
# OF SOMETHING

Eating crisps in an alleyway might not seem like the most sociable thing to be doing on a Saturday night. You may expect people to be out dancing in a club, drinking in a bar with friends, chatting to people at a party or sitting in with a boyfriend or girlfriend watching a cool DVD. But that's normal people and I ain't normal. I'm quite malnormal.

I'll give you a few examples. Last week I fried my watch in a pan for no reason. Two hours later I was wrapped up in my duvet in the bank asking the door for a loan. I've been arrested for trying to shoplift CDs and books and I've been barred from three local hospitals because all the doctors and nurses said they would prefer to see me dead than be irritated by my 'nonsense' anymore. I'm crazy alright, but that sort of treatment really hurts me. I didn't ask to be born fucked. I didn't ask to be born without any arms. I didn't ask to be born inside a jar, dead. Luckily I was only born fucked, mindily, but it has created an a lot amount of problems for me.

So here I am on a drizzly Saturday night in Temple Bar, straightening out the edge of a packet of crisps, tilting my head back, putting the packet to my mouth and letting the crisps slide into it. As I munch on the synthesised cheese and onion flavour I wonder where I'm going to go in life. I look at the other people walking around, bursting with excitement and gaudy laughter. Will I ever be one of these people? Will I ever find that sort of fun? I fold the packet up, stick it behind my ear and suck my greasy fingers clean. There's not really anywhere for me to go so I sit down instead. It's after five in the morning and everyone is pissed. They are walking around like they have the legs of a new born foal.

'Get a job!!' I scream at an eight year old girl shifting some auld lad and give her the fingers. She pushes the old man away and walks over and sits beside me.

'What's wrong with you?' she asks in a sweet young voice.

'I'm fed up of being crazy and lunatic and mad. How come you get to have fun, drinking, shifting, clubbing. You barely look eight!'

'I'm nineteen,' she says rather indignantly. 'Anyway you'll hardly make friends if you just scream at everyone!' I think about this for a second. The old man staggers over and tries to grab the girl away but she stabs him with a small knife. He stumbles and falls backwards into some bin bags, clutching his stomach and wheezing. I think he faints or something then.

'I only scream because I'm so sad inside,' I reply eventually.

'No, you scream because you're angry. Stop being so angry and maybe you'll see how to make friends. Try it out. Here's my phone number, text me in a few weeks and tell me how you're getting on.' She scribbles something on a piece of paper and hands it to me.

'Thank you,' is all I can say.[40]

She stands up, adjusts her top and struts off into the staggering mass of alcohol'd humans with kebabs and white shirts/red faces.

---

40. This is the second last line of my book.

# THE

# END

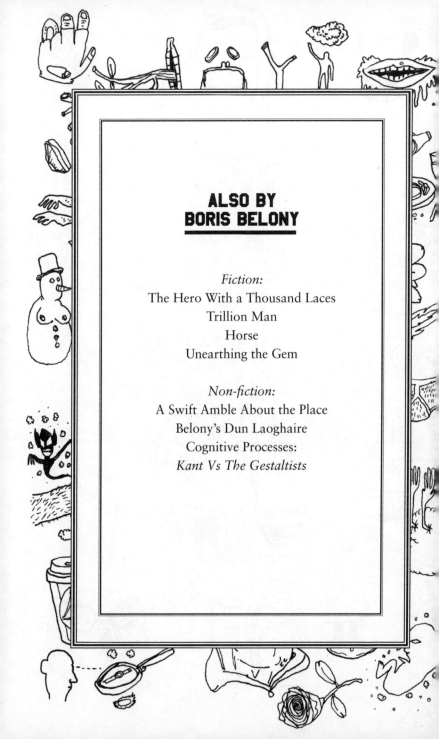

## ALSO BY
## BORIS BELONY

*Fiction:*
The Hero With a Thousand Laces
Trillion Man
Horse
Unearthing the Gem

*Non-fiction:*
A Swift Amble About the Place
Belony's Dun Laoghaire
Cognitive Processes:
*Kant Vs The Gestaltists*

# TRACK LISTING

1. Oh.. OH
2. Hilly
3. The Painting
4. Someone Else
5. Tied Down
6. Sad Soup
7. Black Demise
8. Skydive
9. The Snowflake

*Credits:*
Music composed by Julia Mahon

Boris Belony: Orator
Julia Mahon: Piano
Claire O'Donnell: Harp
Ailbhe Nic Oireachtaigh: Viola, Violin
Patrick Dexter: Cello
Cian Nugent: Saw

Recorded and mixed by Eoin Whitfield
Mastered by James Eager
at The Hive Studios